Rush

Of

Many

Waters

Also by Pauly Hart

Rush of Many Waters:

Volume Twelve

By Pauly Hart

ISBN: 978-1-955399-15-9
Library of Congress Catalog Data is available at: Loc.gov
This book is available at cost on Amazon.com and wherever
fine books are sold.
Front Cover Art by Franz Marc:
Front cover design by Pauly Hart
Paperback version printed in Savannah, Georgia, USA,
where available.
First Edition, 2021
Author Contact: EmpiresAndGenerals@gmail.com
Author Website: PaulyHart.com

Contents

Shorts

Dipping the Green

I guess you can call it "dipping." At least that's what Master Song Lu calls it. "Dipping." One's ability to go down unseen into the subconscious mind of the universe and "see" what goes on underneath. While others talk of the supernatural as if it were something crazy and evil... I was learning the tricks of getting into the whole of those mysteries.

I remember the first time that I met Master Song Lu. I was visiting Teddy at his dojo. Master Lu had been the guest instructor that day, as it was the yearly open house. We walked in on him going one-on-one with Teddy's sensei: Master Cho. He was a black belt in several martial arts forms and was being man-handled like a little girl. Master Song Lu says he is no martial arts expert, he only dabbles a little in Aikido... He says. But that day, he was in "the zone." He says that when you are in that special place - you can see everything that is happening around you before it happens...

At least that is how it was described to me.

Though I was not a member of Teddy's dojo during the open house, they were having what they call an "open floor", and everyone was invited to spar with anyone else. When we arrived, everyone was watching in rapt attention at the performance before us. No one noticed us, except Master Song Lu. As we were walking in, he was watching the door, still sparing with Teddy's instructor. We caught eyes for the briefest of seconds.

Cho was on the mat in two swift moves.

"Dayum!" Teddy hollered, pounding me on the back. "I told you he was good."

Master Cho, exhausted after the combat, but a good sport, hopped to his feet, smiled at Master Song, bowed and pronounced him the winner. Master Cho and Master Song Lu walked over to Teddy and me. Song Lu, was barely five feet and Master Cho, almost six and a half. The other students and visitors took the time to talk and get water or Gatorade. It was the four of us in a crowded room, but the massive vibe that the little man put out made you feel like you were alone with him in the Gobi Desert.

"Ah, Teddy" Master Cho said, "Glad you came. I just got my ass handed to me by this Nip."

"Be careful" said Master Song Lu, "I am only half Japanese. The other parts of me are even worse."

They laughed. I had expected Master Cho to be stuffy and formal, but I see now that his informality was the reason that Teddy kept coming back here. He was pretty cool.

"Hi, I'm Flick" I said. I stuck out my hand at Master Cho. Gripping it with the firmest handshake in North America, he pumped it twice and threw my arm back at me as if he were a dog and had found my arm to be an unsatisfactory bone.

"Master Cho" he said. "And this is Master Song Lu."

"Greetings Flick." he said, and gave a slight nod of his head.

"Song Lu, show Teddy what you showed me." said Master Cho, still rubbing his wrist from where Song Lu had grabbed him.

"Ah. Certainly, if you would like." Master Lu smiled.

"Er. Yeah, prolly gonna hand mah ass to me, but what the hey." Teddy said, popped his shoes off and began stretching.

Teddy and Master Song Lu squared off in the middle of the floor. They bowed to each other. Teddy took the Universal Stance, not understanding how to best defend against the style of Master Song Lu, and not really knowing if there was a defense at all.

Master Song stood, not in a stance, and almost seemed asleep on his feet. He didn't sway, but if you asked me later if I had thought he had - I would have said yes. He was in such a state of peace that you could feel the room melt off of him like butter. Neither one moved for several seconds. Teddy shifted weight a couple of times, trying to throw off Master Song's zen, but to no avail. Master Song Lu did not move.

Suddenly with a flurry of hand flails, Teddy stomped his foot but it was a feint. He stopped short of Master Song by inches and leaped away. The balk was a test.

Master Song Lu still had not moved. Teddy changed to the Renoji-dach stance, back foot sideways, holding most of his weight and front foot out ready for a defensive kick. He was ready... But not for what happened next.

In the deep time of the cosmos, the eons that pass over and wash the skies clean of stars every morning, there is a longing, a thirst, a hunger for the push of anything countable. In the spaces that men know, the moments that we hold of value and the seconds that make up our minutes, there is the fallacy that we call this "time". Time is an uncounted thing, a large rough beast that comes in unwanted and unheeded to our lives and tramples us to dust, nonresistant to our pleas and supplications. A distant and angry god, not to be ignored.

And what happened to Teddy could have only been explained by me stating this concept to you now. For it was as if time itself had bowed low to Song Lu and begged his forgiveness for getting in his way. Time had taken leave of its senses and allowed Master Lu to persuade it of something that it was reticent to allow. In one brief millionth of a second Master Song Lu was on one side of the mat, facing Teddy with his hands by his side. And in the other part of that millionth of a second he was behind Teddy, flipping him over his knee in a take-down. *Wham!* Elbow to the gut, chop to the neck, flat of the arm against the bicep with a slap, then a leap away. It wasn't even a terrific leap, rather average and dull in comparison.

Maybe because he hadn't moved to him the way I thought he had. He had simply materialized behind him. Like Nightcrawler from the X-Men, he had been in one place, in one second, and in another place inside of the same second. Except in this case, there was no large plume of black smoke. How on earth was that possible?

Teddy had hit the mat with an *"Oommph!"* and allowed himself to be taken down, but I am sure that the confusion of the whole matter allowed him to be on the ground longer than it should have. He got up with a shake of the head. *See? What did I tell you?* his face smiled and told us.

Master Song was around the same spot that he had been moments before, and bowed to Teddy. "Oh yeah." Teddy let out. He had been so put off, he had forgotten his manners in the confusion. "Yer turn buddy."

A startled Cho interrupted him. "Oops! Real quick, let's get him some forms." Master Cho hopped around the door into his office. Like most modern Dojo's, the office was just a tiny area off to the side of the large open room, where the action happened. Mats adorned the floor all around, some square but most round. The largest square one was in the approximate shape of a boxing ring. "That's for the Muay Thai Kali guys. They're nuts, but we share the studio with them. They meet on the days that we don't."

Master Lu had made his way over to us as Master Cho was looking for the forms. He was a small man with a large white blouse, and loose fitting black pants. He was smiling at me. "You are ready?" He extended his hand as if the greeting we had earlier hadn't happened.

"Ah, yeah. Can't wait." I said, and extended my hand. His grip was light, almost like a woman's, and yet, you knew you were being held. He didn't shake it really, just held it.

"You have an inner glow." he said, "A Strength. People have told you this?" He asked me.

"Uh, not in so many words. My mom loves me I guess." I said, Teddy laughed. Master Song Lu smiled and winked.

"Love is not to be trifled with." he said.

"Here they are!" Master Cho had arrived from his office in a flurry of loose-leaf madness. Pen in hand like a flaming sword, he pressed it into mine and had me sign the release forms guaranteeing that if I died or was seriously injured, I would not sue the Dojo for every last penny.

I signed, took my shoes off, and squared off with Master Song Lu. Was I stupid or was there something larger at work here than just betting on me getting my ass beat?

We bowed and began.

That was fourteen years ago, if I recall. He had let me dance around him for a while in the ring. Much longer than Cho or Teddy. I didn't have any formal training, just the YMCA boxing league from when I was a kid. But he acted like a beginner. With a smile and his hands he beckoned me to attack, but then when I did it felt like he wasn't really there. It was like he was not really even trying. I couldn't really be angry. Aikido or no Aikido, it was unique. I would punch or kick and the people in the Dojo would applaud half-heartedly, but their hearts weren't in it.

The longer this lasted, the more I began to question it. Not understanding why Master Song Lu was toying with me like that, I became more and more fierce. The longer the fight lasted, the bolder I became. Pretty soon I was attacking him insane full force, and he was blocking and dodging everything.

I knew I was connecting with him from time to time. A solid connection would land, but as soon as my fist or foot would find contact, it would kind of slide off to the side. I thought I did, but I never actually "landed" anything head on, and so he never really was "hit". Around ten minutes into it I was winded from all the "fighting." Hands on knees, I stood there panting, starting to drip from the sweat. He stood over me with his hands behind his back, bowed slightly, smiled and asked: "Ready to begin?"

I shouldn't have, but I nodded 'yes' and went after him.

At the thirty minute mark, he finally put me down on the mat. I was a sweaty red mess of exhaustion. He was pristine. He winked at me, bowed to the crowd and left. Teddy drove me home in silence. Even he didn't know what to make of it all.

They say that the woman who first dreamt up the idea for the new path of Shinto had a dream from Konjin himself... Calling him the Kami that would restore the world. She built the Oomoto sect of Shinto into a thriving enterprise. The Kami possessed her time and time again, giving her speeches, visions, information, and plans. Once, he possessed her for weeks on end and she wrote over two hundred thousand pages, mostly poetry about the return of the human mind to the place of clean water... To the source... To dip into the green.

And that's why he said that he only "dabbled" in Aikido. Because to know it fully would be to know Konjin himself. That was the lie, wasn't it? How does a demon know himself when he has only been alive less than two hundred years? I didn't know what he was doing then, but since then I have been able to piece it together. Each block, each throw, each time he bent away from my kicks and punches, he knew... He was dipping into my soul. Like a wary bird he would dip just a little bit at a time, to get me to go farther and farther into the attacks.

I really can't see the screen any more. My mother says that the font won't get any bigger. Over the last fourteen years I have lost my hearing, my ability to walk, and now my eyesight. The doctors called it Mitochondrial Dysfunction at first. The inability for my cells to use the right fuel source. Now they are using me to feed me. My other maladies the doctors have no answer for, but they do test after test and still come up with no result.

I don't know what will fail next. My kidneys? Liver? I could get a nasty virus and be down for the count at any moment. I've thought about ending it all but my family loves me. Honestly, they have been my only real support. I don't see my old friends anymore, including Teddy. It's hard to get to church and I was never very popular with anyone else. In the end, what Master Song Lu did to me was steal my life. Energy and life are stolen every day, but it's never like it is in the movies. It's never the black caped blood sucking vampire that comes in through your window at midnight. It's not like that at all. "Dipping the green" is what he called it. It was me that he dipped.

As I lay here, all I can really think about is: how long would he last from the energy I fed him?

When will he feed again?

Trentan's Voyage

The valley was almost too dark for Trentan to see. He led his horse down, ever down in... careful not to trip and fall over the rocks that were strewn hither and yon upon the path. At the bottom, there wasn't much. Only a dim river and a queer fog, and an awful smell. That was it. And they said that this is where he would find the prophet. Here of all places.

At the deepest and loneliest part of the valley, he came upon the dwelling. More hovel than house, it seemed to be occupied, for there was a flicker of a light from the inside. Looking in the window but seeing no one within, he opened the door.

A startling voice said: "Leave your horse around back you silly thing! What do you think this is, a barn or something? Hurry up about it!"

Trentan was only fourteen rotations old, but by Kalimsa standards, he was well into his manhood. He knew proper formality and kicked himself mentally for not announcing himself before he had entered. Quickly ducking out, he lashed his beast to a scraggly tree at the rear of the hut, and came back around to the front.

"And don't you dare leave your manners out in that fog either!" the voice said.

With that, he entered the hut.

The next morning Trentan stared at the newly rising sun. It had been glowing strangely for several rotations. The star lookers had not been able to explain the reddish glow pulsating every eleven days or so about it, it had scared the young and old alike in his home village. The landscape had been the most affected by the sun's abnormalities. The scrub-trees were all but dead, and most of the fruit plants had withered and stopped producing. Trentan, still alone in his thoughts, had not noticed Torq, the oldest of the star-lookers, and owner of the hovel, now standing beside him.

"You know it's quite beautiful, if you think about it." said Torq.

"Yes, but who wants to do that?" replied Trentan. "All I can see is that our world is being eaten up by that monster, and there's nothing we can do about it."

"Ah Trentan, always to the point. Yes, you're right my son, eaten up, and eventually destroyed. We are dying yes? The planet is drying up... all is going the way of the blood sea... but who said that we could do nothing?" Torq's quick eye peered at him.

"Well, what is there to do? We have no majik. Our powers died when the greats were lost to the Omicron. Now our powers are gone. And my father says that we will perish like they did... so long ago."

"Oh, your father's a fortune teller, is he?"

"N... No, but you know he is third-breeder in Kalimsa."

"Oh, I understand. He has seen the way that the bulls are mating recently and has ascertained that by divine understanding, this year will be the beginning of the end... Just because some rhys couldn't perform? Hmm? Yes, I'm sure that he understands all of the complexities of the Majik of nature..." Torq trailed off.

"What?" Trentan asked incredulously and shook his head. "My father says that there is no power in nature anymore. Hashir is dead to us. She has been like a fickle whore, and has now sought after other lovers than us. Perhaps she dwells with the Omicron now... My father says there is no more power in Hashir. There is only power in might and the edge of the sword."

Torq looked away disgusted. In the heavens he had always sought his answer. The stars were beginning to fade with the rise of the sun. But the stars, they were his friends, and had always been so. But recently they had shut him out. The sky had become the enemy to all. Besides, what did this old man know?

"My father says this, my father says that." Torq looked over at Trentan. "Is that all you can say? Don't you have anything to say on your own? My boy, the time has come for you to start having your own ideas in these matters." Torq paused and looked once again at the sun-scape. "Come with me, I want to show you something."

He led Trentan down the long slope that connected to the dusty plain. The rhys had long since been moved into more shady areas to graze... but these had been shrinking steadily since the drought began. The herders had begun to graze at night and let the herds sleep during the day. The sun was making them sick, and the trees and the land.

Torq commented on this. "The heat is unbearable for our herds isn't it?"

"Yes." Trentan said.

Torq continued, "Isn't it strange that we have not been affected by the sun in the same way that the land has?" He probed.

Trentan stopped. "I hadn't really thought about it... I wonder why?"

"Oh, no one has Trentan. No one even wants to consider the possibility. Rotation after rotation, all of Hashir is dying ever so slowly... but we do not!" Torq rants, still walking. "No one wants to hear it! All are deaf to what I have to say. Bah! Incompetents! Come Trentan, I don't have any more use for them. They think I am crazy. They don't even listen to wisdom. I am surprised that your village elder sent anyone to see me at all!"

Trentan thought about that. It had been strange when they had called him in from the field with the request to go to the old seer's home and get instruction. Was the need so great that they had changed into more drastic measures?

Trentan had to run to catch up. "Why is it that they do not respect you? Aren't you the oldest of the Star-lookers?"

"Ha!" Torq spat with obvious contempt. "Yes, and they want me to die. They wish I would take that long journey into the far away. Trentan, they hate me. All of them. But who will have the last laugh I wonder?"

Trentan had no comment. As they walked, he noticed that the newly risen sun had a more sickly pallor to it than it did days earlier... or even yesterday. It did, didn't it? Perhaps it was all in his mind. Talking to Torq was like being made to eat razor-berries, but the sun still. It really did look much worse than he had ever seen it.

"Torq." He said, "I'm curious about..."

"Quiet!" Torq snapped. "No more talking! If you're so curious, then shut your pipe and follow me. It's time to walk."

Trentan did as he was told. Though he really had no intention of following Torq around all day. He knew that the old sage could get crabby sometimes. Torq had always liked Trentan for some reason hidden from Trentan. As a boy, when Torq would visit, he would follow the old man around when all of his school mates were playing ball.

He had always had Torq's eye, but was never interested in continuing his education with the old grump. After his schooling was finished he had gone to work for his father, and that was that. But Torq would check in on him from time to time. Always asking questions of Trentan's dreams, his adventures, his aspirations and views on different subjects. Trentan knew Torq, and he knew that this was a bad time to open his mouth full of idle chatter.

It wasn't long until Trentan understood where they were going. There were several myths about the great ones. One is that, using majik, they had created a vast and fertile paradise where they had lived for hundreds of rotations, but when the swarm came all of it had been destroyed and was now lost forever. Before they left however, they stored all of their vast knowledge in a pyramid shaped structure that Trentan's people called Trialythe Darco.

For generations, scholars had come to Trialythe Darco to try and decipher the ancient's texts and make some sense of the patterns in and around the actual pyramid. Scholars, Majiks, Mystiks, Peasants and Kings alike had all come, but no one had ever succeeded. And if Torq thought to uncover the secrets now... Trentan thought, he would surely fail just like all the rest. But what did he know? Perhaps Torq had solved all the secrets. If he did, would he have told anyone? Just how much did Trentan know about this ancient star-looker who plodded along ahead of him. Not much at all.

Not much had ever been learned of the Darco. Actually nothing. There was a maze cut into the rock all around it, glyphs carved into the Darco itself, and into the maze surrounding. On the outskirts of the great maze stood seven pillars on which one could stand and see the entire structure. One night Trentan had stolen away from his work after putting the rhys in their pen and had ridden all night to come up on one of the pillars and gazed at the stars until he had slept. He dreamt so vividly that night and it scared him so badly that he rode back home early in the morning before anyone had noticed that he was gone. He had never been back.

They had walked all morning long. What he thought had been a quick look-see at something a quick walk away had turned into a two-hand march. It was coming up on three. The red sun hung in the sky like a globe of fury. Sweat dripped down Trentan's brow and he wondered if he was as crazy as the old man. They had not rested and the conversation had been terse and sporadic. Trentan's mind was no longer on the sky, it was on food.

"Did you break fast before we left, young one?" the wizened sky watcher asked him, as if reading his mind.

That brought him up short. "Uh... no, actually I was just wondering if..."

"Good! Good indeed. No food! No rest! Come, come; plenty of walking will help you forget the complexities of your make-up. Food does not cleanse, only revitalizes. Emptiness is close to cleanliness And right now, purity is of more importance than energy." Torq harrumphed and shook off some dust from his robes and started walking again.

They walked all day.

He was thirsty. He was hungry. He was tired. He was delirious. The sun was almost set and Torq had not stopped, or even given Trentan a reason for this expedition. He kept wondering about his father and what he was going to say to him when they returned. He hadn't said goodbye. Nothing. He had seen the Village Elder and had taken off immediately last night.

He was sure to be in for a good lashing. This was not going to be something he looked forward to. The thoughts running through his head for the most part entailed Torq in several torture positions. Maybe a rack with a good stretch, Or butter on the stomach and a room full of Slarva-rats. Suddenly, Torq went crazy.

"Consequence!" Torq screamed, and stood motionless. Trentan was so thirsty and light-headed that he wasn't sure that he was imagining that he was seeing the old fool up on a flat rock yelling at the wind.

"Consequence and recrimination! These are two! Are there not more?"

His mind reeled and all of the organs in his body cramped as one. Tissues that had not been used since the days he was pre-born remembered their purpose and seized. Bile that was safely inside of his stomach began to make its way up and into his mouth. His legs and arms and shoulders cramped and spasmed violently. Was it dehydration or something else? His vision flashed white and then darkened, like a tunnel, and then was clear again.

Torq was on top of a flat rock. Looking around, he was not surprised to see that he had not gone completely out of his mind. They were at the monolith. They had arrived at Trialythe Darco. So if he wasn't imagining this, then why was Torq screaming? He was sure that the cobwebs in Torq's frail mind had caught some insect of insanity and had finally snapped. Until he heard another voice.

"Justice and equality! These are two! Are there not more?"

All around the monolith in a perfect circle were outcroppings of evenly spaced teeth. In between these, were platforms, like the one that he and Torq were standing on now. It was a drop inside of the circular area to the monolith, farther than he could throw a rock and it was quite a drop as well. The monolith looked to be 100 hands high and the tip of it was eye level with the top of the teeth around them. Although he could not see the other side of the ridge, he could hear what was being said perfectly. Some creation in the way the sound worked, made everything crystal clear, and as the wizards (or whatever they were, for Trentan had given up on making sense of the whole ordeal) shouted out platitudes and apparent philosophy to each other... the rocks around them began to take on a pinkish hue. A trick? No, it was something more.

On and on they had droned with the setting sun and his mind droned and hummed along with the sounds. Deliverance. Mercy. Hope. Liberty. He almost knew the words before they were spoken. And as he recalled, some of the voices, he hadn't been able to understand at all. He had figured them for Anganosian, yet he knew he had heard everything plainly.

And then the shouting stopped. Unbelievably, the monolith began to glow. In a perfect bowl, the monolith sat at the very middle. Black as night with odd carvings, whorls and designs, it was now almost hypnotic to look at. Yellowish-gold sparks raced along the designs. Then ground underneath began to shake almost imperceptibly.

At least it was imperceptible at first. As it rose in force, it became clearer that the floor of the bowl was cleansing itself. For so long, it had sat neglected. Now it was alive. Sand and dust, Pebbles and rock acted as one and began blowing/crawling/rolling/drifting away from the plain. Spaces to the left and right of Trentan began to fill with the rock. There was a howling and there was nothing he could do but drop down and lie still hoping that this upside-down landslide wouldn't carry him away in its wake.

He was on his hands and knees. Not wishing to show fear, but as the same time not wishing to fall into the now river of earth rushing by on either side of him. The platform was safe and gave him a perfect vista as the floor of the plain began to take shape.

There was a perfect circle around the monolith. At what appeared seven points, there was a peak with a flat rock raised up and just enough room for four men to stand upon. All over the peak where he and Torq were, were similar designs as those on the monolith. They also glowed. What appeared as sparks on the monolith, when viewed closer were nothing more than odd traces of light. If Trentan tried to look too closely at one, it would disappear. He found that if he was not trying to look at any one specific one, he could see them all. He tried not to look.

The floor had transformed itself. The grass was gone and now the floor was completely black. Blanketing the entire floor was a design so complex, he wondered how anyone had ever had the scope to design it without star tools. But of course that's what they used. He was foolish. Foolish and alone. Alone? Where was Torq? There he was just walking down into the whole array. Where in the name of heavens was he going? Who knew? He jumped down and was right behind him.

There were six more Wizards. Seven including Torq the old star watcher. Trentan followed him down into the mess of whorls and patterns that glowed and glistened black as the approaching night. No longer tired or hungry, he had been fueled with the power of the place. Torq seemed to grow larger the more steps that he took down. Really he did not increase in size at all, it just seemed that way. This was not so strange in and of itself, although you would think that is would be. But with the whole spectacle of weirdness going on around him, Trentan did not think it was an odd thing at all.

When they reached the bottom of the slope, Torq stopped and waited. Then, taking his hands and his staff, he began tracing odd patterns in the air. Slowly, but steadily, a wall appeared. It was blue hued and covered the circular plain like a hen covers her eggs. Torq tapped his left pinky finger on it once and a door-frame appeared. He traced in the air some more, and spoke this:

> From the dawn of all time,
> To the rising of the new,
> In the worlds without end,
> your power does remain.
> In the seams of all lives,
> Lies the crevice of truth,
> And the coming of you,

Like a thief in the night.

The door opened; Torq went through and Trentan rushed in behind him.

Upon going through the door, three things happened at once. First of all Trentan experienced a rush like no other before. It was as if electricity had been placed inside of his head and he had swallowed fire, and been submerged into a cave of Noggay bats all at the same time. He literally buzzed with energy. Secondly, his vision depth perception switched. Things that were far away became closer and thee things that were close were... no that's not right... The wizards were all large, and the distance between them had shrunk... No, that wasn't right either.

Well, at any rate, what he saw was this: Each wizard had adorned himself with a robe of astounding color. Brilliant greens, yellows, oranges; all much too bright to look at. Even Torq had taken a midnight blue robe from somewhere. Perhaps it was the same robe, but it was not important. What was important however was the size of things. What appeared to be the plain of the monolith drifted between the seven wizards. It was perhaps only a finger's width high, and the plain was the size of a table, and the others were standing all around it. This was very strange until Trentan noticed the third thing. He was standing outside of his body.

He tried not to be too upset about this, but the more he thought of it, the more it bothered him. He stood there looking (almost) down at himself as he stood behind Torq. This could get confusing, so he tried to explain it to himself this way:

Trentan #1 is his consciousness.

Trentan #2 is the body located behind Torq.

This helped him immensely. #1 floated about the "room", which wasn't a room at all seeing that they were outside, and looked at the faces of the others. He was surprised to see a Romodian and a Anganosian there, but what really got his attention was the Leviathan. Behind each of them was another figure. Trentan didn't know how he hadn't noticed this before, but it was after all a very strange day. The figures for the most part were younger men (and the odd leviathan) and they were situated behind each of the seven wizards. Trentan included himself in this equation, just for the ease of it all. Fourteen people. Seven old and now mumbling, and seven younger and standing (or floating) behind them.

The wizards were singing and humming ancient words. Each of them working their hands in downward and then upward circles, and then odd figures in the air. They began slowly walking in circles. Trentan #2 and the rest of the other companions stood mutely behind them. This was the first time he had seen their faces. Young, energetic, and apparently full of comprehension as to what was going on. He noticed #2's face. Frightened and alone and not understanding.

He wished to make that face brave. He tried but could not. Somehow he was detached and he had no control over what was to happen next. As he floated above the odd scenario, he noticed the position of the sun. The last rays were coming in over the ridge and keying in on the peak of the monolith. Just as he looked down/up at the tip, the last sunrays of the day touched it and the monolith exploded.

"*Owww!*" Trentan groaned as he tried to get up. The blood rushed to his head and he heard a sound like the tide against the rocks. Light was streaming in on him, although he wasn't able to comprehend where it came from. He smelt something like fish cooking.

"Good day to you dreamer!" came the annoyingly cheery voice. "Did you sleep well?"

"*Ugh.*" He grumbled. "What time is it?"

"Around one" Torq stated, referring to a hands breadth from the time of sunrise. "You overslept, young one... No matter, you remember last night, yes?"

"Of course... I was there."

"No! Too much thinking! Were you theeeeeere?" He cocked his head and gleamed at him. Trentan, not fully awake yet, didn't understand. Was he there? Of course! The way he had been separated from himself, was this what Torq was referring to?

"I remember floating..." It was slowly coming back to him. "Yes, I remember floating, and you and the rest were suspended, and there was chanting and then... Oh! there was a leviathan!"

After Torq finished laughing, he explained it all to him.

Poems

Sugar

Sugar my soul

Savior so sweet

Enhance my joy

Lover of dreams

Ignite my fire

Killer of dark

Spring on me

Bringer of smiles

Satisfy souls

Jesus of mine

Tragedy on Kankakee

there i was on the river
tragedy and midgets
that's all i remember
fernando was trapped under
that damned log again
except this time...

we couldn't get him out
mike was accusing everyone
of killing the poor bastard
but as james informed me
shit happens everyday
and midgets die

just like the rest of us.

Little Girl

You are a little girl
shrouded in beauty
enwrapped in mystery
yet you love me
because i am nice

i don't understand
why you care so much
for a little boy like me
when you have all yourself
to worry about everyday

You are alluring
A countess
A mysterious charmer
that vexes my heart bare

I am nothing you need
I am small and impure
I will hurt you
If you come too close

Yet you smile
and wiggle your toes
when i make you laugh

with my stories

Why do you love me
little girl?

Evangelist

Evangelist, Evangelist.
Come blow your horn.

Evangelist, Evangelist.
is stuck on porn.

Evangelist, Evangelist.
Take all our funds.

Evangelist, Evangelist.
Is on the run.

Evangelist.
Blow in.

Evangelist.
Blow up.

Evangelist.
Blow out.

Who cleans up your mess,
Oh mighty Evangelist?

`help!`

The bell tolled.

I picked the sunflowers.
    I threw the box away.
The cock crowed.
    I looked at jewelry.
        I washed the dirty dishes.
The water boiled.
    I memorized Chinese.
        I asked for help.
Help was given.
    I ate my lunch.
        I asked for help.
Help was given.
    I drove to town.
        I asked for help.
Help was given again.
    I worked all day.
        I asked for help.
More help was given.
    I came home at night.
        I cried for help.
Help was there.
    I opened my ears.
        Help was there.
The bell tolled.
    I recognized the help.
        I said "thank you".

Waiting and waiting

The fountain of joy overflows so near to my heart,
    For I am here waiting for you.
The flowers of springtime bloom even at dark,
    And I am here waiting for you.
A lovelier person I have never once met,
    Still I am here waiting for you.
And a richer secret have I never yet kept,

So I am here waiting for you.
The sweetest aroma of your loves desire,
   While I am here waiting for you.
Burns deeply inside like a holy fire,
   For I am here waiting for you.
The Spirit of giving, His coal to my lips,
   And I am here waiting for you.
Your precious blood cleansing our relationship,
   So I am here waiting for you.
A cloud by the daytime shown forth in the sun,
   While I am here waiting for you.
A fire by the night for our work's almost done,
   Still I am here waiting for you.
No sweeter love yet has this man ever seen,
   Still I am here waiting for you.
Your true heart I've kept by emotional strings,

   I thank you for waiting for me.

Resistance

When the other prophets are saying the same thing that is not truth.
Micaiah said "As surly as God lives, I can only speak what is truth."

And Zedikiah will you now slap God in the face for bearing the truth?
For the Lord is One and the evil spirit He placed in you was not truth.

Israel says to Judah, "Here is one who hates me as well as the truth."
False prophets echoing your own personal desires is not reality truth.

Reality is the fact that all things just and pure resistant all non - truth.
Ahab, now as you are pulled from battle you realize that there is truth.

Now your son will fall to his death
His kingdom will be devoured in flames.

And your lineage will not pass from him.
For resistance to truth is suicide.

Poor, poor Zedikiah.

Spontaneous Psalm #13

Oh I pray for America
And the land of the free
May freedom not cover us
But let us be covered by thee

I pray for the children
Of those both near and far
I pray for the healing
From hearts cold and hard

And I pray for my people
Both lost and abused
I asked for your mercy
Lord pour out your news

Good news of the freedom
Good news of the cross
Good news of the one who died
On calvary

I pray for the children
Both dead now and lost
Lord comfort their mothers
Those used and sights lost

I pray for the fathers
Turn now their hearts
Oh back to their children
To never depart

Good news of you Jesus
Good news of the cross
That was for me
Good news of the blood
That flowed down calvarys tree

And I pray for the children
And I pray for us children
And I pray for you children
That you would be free

Essays

The Littlest Rebel

You know what's fun? Waking up one day and realizing that all of your friends think you're insane. Soon after my baptism, I was moved to a private school. Make no mistake, I was a problem child and was moved around every couple of years. It was easier to do it this way than try to reform the hooligan that was Mister Pauly Hart. At the first private school I went to we had an actual "Religion Class" where we learned all about the fabulous Martin Luther and how he started the Reformation Movement. It was pretty cool. Very structural and methodical but there was still room in my heart for the non-metaphorical Christ. It was just harder to find Him inside of all the organized religion that was presented to me. The Lutherans had a very different viewpoint on the working hand of God than the Baptists or Charismatics.

This doesn't mean I didn't try my hardest to get my questions answered. I would come up with some zingers and they wouldn't have a clue what to do with them. You want to really annoy a dead religious people's ethos, you start asking them about a living and active Creator. Oh boy, watch out. There's no one more defensive than a religious guy who "knows" he's right. And, of course, when I transferred to yet another school, the same thing happened. So I went to 4th-6th at a private Lutheran school and 7-10th (my parents stepped up their game) they sent me to a Mennonite Academy out in the middle of nowhere. Dress code and all that - Yargh. It was even more strict. Still had a "Religion Class" but at least we talked about more than Luther. Chapel was often fun. But my Religion teacher often sent me to the Principal's office (or the Superintendent if he was really in a bad mood.) Once he told us that if he didn't believe him on a subject, we could look it up in the dictionary! So I got out of my seat and got the dictionary on his desk. Yes, another trip to the Principal's office.

Why you gotta kill the child for a desire to learn? I don't know. The only thing I came away from that school with was some good stories. Religion it seemed, was lost on me. But only at school. Home life, was another matter altogether. I am an introvert. I don't like crowds, I don't like parties, I don't like mixers, I don't like groups. I don't generally like people. As I am writing this I look to the other laptop beside me where "Alone" Season 3 is queued up ready to play. "If only…" I sigh. Such is the mind of me: A hermit and a weirdo by choice and by blessing. The fact that I live with another introvert as her husband is an irony seldom lost on me. But let me rewind. From a young age all I ever wanted to do was play with Legos and read comics. Reading and building fantasy worlds led me quickly into Role Playing Games where I could be a ninja thief who could steal jewels and slay dragons. The fantasy world had been often larger than the real one. My dad would have none of this and thrust me into Boy Scouts to enlarge my mind and rectify my moral compass.

So in Boy Scouts, (guess what Dad) we played Role Playing games and read comics. Anything that had to do with outer space, wizards, Martians and warlocks was within bounds. And I loved every moment of it. Marvel Comics and Palladium Role Playing Games when I was forced to be on the bus ride home or at Boy Scouts, and when I was alone? It was H.G. Wells and DC Comics. Nothing was better than Saturday when I could watch Transformers, G.I. Joe, Super Friends, Space Ghost and Flash Gordon. And, if I wasn't in the mood for re-runs I would get by with Spider-Man, Hulk and Shazam. But I would relive those fantasy worlds all weekend long and straight into the next week. As long as it didn't have anything to do with reality and relied heavily on deep Science Fiction, I was into it.

The Artist and the Island

Throughout all of my wanderings I had finally decided to quit messing around with my life and become an artist. I painted, made music, sang, directed a drama, danced, played percussion, wrote poetry, wrote essays, short stories, and just recently, a novel. Most of my work was comprised of poetry and mixed media abstract expression paintings. I bought supplies and sold them for cheap. It was fun but didn't pay the bills. I tried very hard to reason within myself that I should only pursue the callings of God within my heart and the money would come on its own. This sure sounds great but when you have to pay the gas bill and you have no money for groceries, you begin to doubt yourself. So I took side jobs, here and there to make ends meet. I cried within myself: "But I only want to create beauty!" Well, my wallet had a different song it wanted to sing to me. At the end of my wit and my rope I got a job working for Dish Network.

I wasn't an installer, I was a tech who sat at a desk and solved problems over the phone with installers. It was great. They paid well, offered unlimited overtime and eventually I got to be on an Oracle software test team. Our tests were outrageous. We had to learn so much technical data about satellites and dishes and powered cables and hardware, It would rock the mind of an average man. Testing into a higher category was always promoted so I took and passed my "Tech 2" test with some ease. But the more I questioned the weird stuff, the more I was told to look away. We would get "Sun Spot Alerts" every so often that would have no correlation from NOAA and NASA. Having unlimited access to the internet and intranet tools was huge. I was actually proving, little by little, that there were no satellites. It was disheartening and mind-blowing all at once. The data being sent was from large sending dishes that bounced information off of (what I thought at the time) the ozone layer. In reality, I would discern that it was the dome that they were shooting up at. Again, very mind blowing. It was hard and tedious work and I quickly grew tired of it. After having accrued $10,000 in savings and secured stocks I decided that I would pack up my bags and move to the Virgin Islands.

I had accumulated a lot of artwork at the time that I eventually gave away. I had been living at a sound recording studio and gifted it to them. They were happy with that and I was a little sad to let it all go, but I had to skinny down my belongings if I wanted to move to the Caribbean.

So there I was LITERALLY sweating to death, suitcase in hand, and ready to move into my new apartment when it all fell thru. My new roommate had cancelled our plans without telling me and I had nowhere to go. I don't know how I survived those first few weeks but I eventually found a place to stay, secured a job, and found a couple of people I could trust as friends. I had it easy. Working at one of the largest resorts I became the Beach Manager very quickly and had some side ventures as a snorkel instructor and ocean kayak instructor. The pay was good and I got tipped in bottles of alcohol and sex... Well... Sex offers. I turned them all down, remaining chaste. There was really no one I wanted to give it up to. I would rather remain pure, so I did, which only made me even more desirable. Kind of a catch-22, but I trusted God and things turned out OK.

Since island life is a step away from anything I had ever known, it was a very strange adjustment and took a great deal of time. I won't bore you with a lot of the details of my entire time there, but let me interest you in my primary daytime activity which I will simply call: "Horizon Gazing." Besides having enough time to write a couple of books, I would stroll around the island, or drive in and around access points to all the beaches that I could find. I probably took a thousand pictures a month (mostly garbage,) but some of my better ones involved ships, horizons, and my zoom lens. I noticed how, with my naked eye I could see the ship somewhat disappear near the horizon, but when I would zoom in with my camera, the bottom hull would reappear. I never questioned this. At that time in 2006 I was probably a 90% flat earth believer, so I just knew that if I could get a larger zoom power, eventually I would be able to see Africa... Which turned out not to be so far-fetched.

It so happens that, on a clear day, you can see the lights in the buildings of Charlotte Amalie St. Thomas. During the daytime, with a telescope, you can easily see Blackbeard's Castle, but that's on a hill. I mean down at the actual floor of sea-level. You can see lights in hotels, casinos and bars from 42 and a half miles away if you sitting at Christopher Columbus' Landing Site on Salt River Bay at St. Croix. That's insane. According to an earth curvature calculator, you should be missing 1,208 feet of view, maybe enough to see Blackbeard's Castle, but not enough to see the boardwalk. It's a well-known fact to everyone who lives on St. Croix (from all those I encountered) that visibility on the ocean only depends on how much money you can spend. During clear days, eastward at Point Udall, you can see the dust coming from the Sahara Desert across the ocean. Going east to Senegal is 3150 miles (2738 nautical) – that's an incredible distance for that dust to travel. I don't know at what point you can see it, but I was blown away each time I would look at the big brown cloud to the east. Now tell me that with 5,809,618 feet of curvature, I would still be able to see it? Even if it travels up into the atmosphere past the supposed maximum of 20,000 feet, it would still not be three inches above the horizon line as it appears to the naked eye at the east end of St. Croix. After I ran out of money, I eventually left the island and moved back to the mainland. I had some fun and met some people, wrote some words and took some pictures. It would not be until later that I would realize that I had some tangible proof of the flat earth.

Mortal life is never enough

Mortal life is never enough pt. 1

i start off in a second story of a condominium that looks strangely like linda and dads second floor of their house. i am helping gg. through a personal crisis, because she got drunk one night and had someone shoot at her who had never held a gun before. she was as calm as a cucumber in a fridge. of course she gets tragic news and proceeds to get me to offer to her that she can shoot at me three times. so i agree with all humility and of course then she has this browning semi auto sniper rifle with out a scope, but i am only like 35 feet away, and there are people watching. the kind of awkward friends you only see in the movies. and only one dark haired girl is trying to pull me away from the wall where i have offered myself up to be shot, just to sooth someone's nerves. so gg is confident but she still has that terrible sadness in her eyes-soul eyes, and she takes two practice shots of to her left, and just can't seem to squeeze off the third round at me, but shoots that to the left as well. Whew! i am thinking, but it didn't seem to be that big of a deal to me at the time... just something i was relieved to get over with. so gg puts the gun down and people are having really different reactions to the whole thing, and i give her this really big hug... so we sit down and have this really in depth discussion about her mom and all of her childhood fears, and all of those kinds of things. so then i am downstairs in some boring cafeteria of a college or magnet school, and it is the type of place where like the geeks and the hard-core study people would want to be... and i am with the same people who were upstairs, and everybody is talking about it and everything is going cool, but that same dark haired girl is sitting at the table in front of my own table talking with a couple of real losers that are manipulating her in believing something on an odd schematic or blueprint, so everyone in the cafeteria is doing something on their own, except for me (where i am really sizing up this situation quite well). so i get my things and go over to where they are and talk her out of all of this really stupid stuff that these two guys were talking about. and then the conversation changes and we talk about what had happened upstairs and how she thought i was really brave and all.

Mortal life is never enough pt. 2

but as i am walking outside i start to notice how this really was a crappy school, and how it is dusk outside, where i was in a sunlit room not an hour ago. and myself and two guys... the same two that were there upstairs, and who i sat next to at the cafeteria, but the two weird guys who i saved the girl from and also gg are nowhere near, and i can only suppose that they are going about their own separate lives now. however i am aware that the short girl is somewhere behind me and to my left because i can hear her talking. so we come upon this massive thing that used to be a parking lot, and it looks like steven speilberg spent $500,000 on art direction on yet another mad max film, or somewhere odd in some strange future of a violent earth... but cars are overturned and there are fires in barrels for warmth, but i am noticing that it is not at all cold. so we are walking along and i am saying hey, i almost bought one of those hats for school, and i say this because there are a whole bunch of guys wearing those black pullover winter hats, and at the same time there are a bunch of guys wearing bright hunter orange ones. but then is when i notice that they are two gangs... so it is really odd that they are all hanging out together and socializing. note: apparently the store where they got their hats ran out of the orange ones and so there are like eight or so out of the 200 members wearing red. or at least that's what i think they are wearing them for. so i am spending an hour or so walking around and talking to people except my clothes have changed. i really had no idea what i was wearing before, but now i am wearing one of those long frock coats worn by the clergy of the late 1800's. i am giving people the news about my experience almost getting shot, and i seem to have a lot of respect of the gang members.

Mortal life is never enough pt. 3

so now four of my fast new gang member friends (but they really appear to be old high school friends that i just associate with much) have taken the burnt-out walmart across the street hostage. but the odd thing is, is that they are up on the roof with a bomb or something, and everyone is really freaked out about it except for me, and i am seemingly quite oblivious to the whole walmart crisis, even though the parking lot is not setup right and we are about seventy feet out in front of the store in the grass, and i am picking these really nice knives up from around one of the pine trees; latino in style, and hand crafted; when one comes whizzing by my chest and lands with a distinct *plunct* sound in the dirt. everyone then springs into action and tries to get me to safety, but only results in walking me around the tree about ten feet to the back, where i walk up to the building and begin demanding where they thought they were and what they thought they were doing... and then telling them that what they thought they were standing for was wrong... but by this time there is this huge barricade behind me with TOO MANY spectators that could be hurt, and so i talk the gang leader down (these types have no hats except black fedoras) and leading him to Christ then and there. he is beaming and the cops/crowd cheer with delight as either i tell him to go home or he does so willingly, and is not arrested... so his three friends do the same thing, and i am the hero. the crowd is amazed again at my bravery, only because as i was walking and talking to these folks up on the roof of the burnt-out super store, the whole lot of 'em on the roof were chucking all of these seemingly antique knives at me. all the while the leech-friends are whimpering and jumping down behind me. they do not seem to have a lick of backbone in the whole lot of them. hmmm, something else that i noticed: the girl seems to have disappeared.

Mortal life is never enough pt. 4

so i am going home because i am very tired of being brave, and come home to our little chateau on a yacht, and my wife and the kids are there... oddly enough i never see the kids in our rooms, which coincidently we share with two older women who are our odd relation... they seem to think that they are somehow our moms, and they keep trying to take care of us... but she and i live in like this two room bedroom conglomeration and there are like shared bathrooms and shared kitchen utilities on this thing, and apparently we never keep our doors locked because these pesky women are ALWAYS coming in and talking to us and seeing what we are doing... which led her and i to start using separate beds... my bed is made up of this huge basin, and it is full of like three inches of water, and i am supported on three air mattresses, and i neither of us can ever get the stupid thing working right... but then her bed is just a couple of blankets all folded up weird, that keep getting wet. and so i try and fix my bed from leaking on the floor, but i can't and just end up making her bed all the more wet, because our beds are only a foot and a half apart. so, she has to go and run errands, with the kids... who i believe are invisible, because i can always tell that they are there, but never actually SEE them... so i take a nap and awaken when she returns, only to find this really cute kids valentines stuck in the kids' door. (they have one of those nursery split-doors.) it says in some weird code that she has left me for jess. so here is the deal, i am really depressed about the whole note thing, and these ladies are bugging me about trying to get you back, and all i really want to do is sleep. however, sleeping on this yacht is something of a torture. There are only four bunks in the downstairs cabin, and they are made of an old pew-like wood. They measure a width of two feet each... wow. that would be hard to sleep on.

www.ingramcontent.com/pod-product-compliance
Lightning Source LLC
Chambersburg PA
CBHW030153200626
46812CB00016B/1828